This book belongs to:

_____

To Harriet
with love from Uncle David

A catalogue record for this book is available
from the British Library

Published by Ladybird Books Ltd
A subsidiary of the Penguin Group
A Pearson Company

LADYBIRD and the device of a Ladybird are trademarks of
Ladybird Books Ltd Loughborough Leicestershire UK

First published by Ladybird Books Ltd MCMXCVI This edition MCMXCVII

Edward
goes exploring

David Pace

Edward loved animals...

and more than anything else in the world he
wanted to be the first to discover a *new* animal.

So one day…

Edward set out into the wild to see what
he could find.

He hadn't gone very far when he heard
a SQUEAKING and a RUSTLING in the big
green bush...

"Ah-haaa!" said Edward. "What's this?
I have discovered some Weenynibbles."

"SQUEEAK! SQUEEAK! We aren't Weenynibbles, we're mice!" squeaked the mice.

So Edward wrote a note in his book: mice

A little further on Edward heard a CROAK, CROAK, CROAKING from down by the pond.

"Ah-haaa!" said Edward. "What's this?
I have discovered some Croakyjumpers."

"CROAK, CROAK! We aren't Croakyjumpers,
we're frogs!" croaked the frogs.

So Edward wrote a note in his book: frogs

Next Edward heard a HISS, HISS, HISSING,
high up in the branches of an old apple tree.

"Ah-haaa!" said Edward. "What's this?
I have discovered a Slitheryslip."

"Hissssssssssss, I'm not a Slitheryslip,
I'm a snake!" hissed the snake.

So Edward wrote a note in his book: snake

Then Edward heard a QUACK, QUACK, QUACKING from down among the reeds.

"Ah-haaa!" said Edward. "What's this? I have discovered some Puddlequackers."

"QUAAACK, QUAAACK! We aren't
Puddlequackers, we're ducks!" quacked the ducks.

So Edward wrote a note in his book: **ducks**

A little further on Edward heard a MEWING and a MIAOWING from behind a tree.

"Ah-haaa!" said Edward. "What's this? I have discovered a Tiggamog."

"MIAOOOOOW! I'm not a Tiggamog, I'm a cat!" miaowed the cat.

So Edward wrote a note in his book: cat

Then Edward heard a WOOF, WOOF, WOOFING from behind a wall.

"Ah-haaa!" said Edward. "What's this? I have discovered a Waggywoof."

"WOOF, WOOF! I'm not a Waggywoof,
I'm a dog!" barked the dog.

So Edward wrote a note in his book: **dog**

Then Edward heard a very, very, very soft
CHOMP, CHOMP, CHOMPING.

"Ah-haaa!" whispered Edward. "What's this?
I have discovered a Leafchomper!"

"CHOMP, CHOMP! I'm not a Leafchomper, I'm a caterpillar," said the caterpillar in a small voice.

So Edward wrote a note in his book:
caterpillar

YOMP CHOMP

CHOMP CHOMP CHOM

Suddenly Edward heard...

A SQUEAKING, a RUSTLING and a CROAK, CROAK, CROAKING. A HISS, HISS, HISSING and a QUACK, QUACK, QUACKING. A MEWING, a MIAOWING and a WOOF, WOOF, WOOFING and a very, very, very soft CHOMP CHOMP CHOMPING.

And… the strangest sound of all.

"Ah-haaa!" said Edward. "What's this?
I have discovered a Splosherwasher!"

"I'm not a Splosherwasher! I'm a Mum!"
said Edward's mum. "And I have discovered
an Edward who needs a bath!"

Then Mum wrote a note in Edward's book:

Bath!